I'm a *Princess*
That Ran Away to A Magical World

written by
Terry Bartley

Contents

1. Obedience and Opposition — 1

2. Out of the Fey Realm — 17

3. A Life of Adventure — 31

4. Freaks Have to Stick Together — 42

5. A Dragon in the Sewer — 48

6. Picking Up the Pieces — 57

7. Would That Really Be So Bad? — 66

8. For the Rest of Your Life — 78

9. Keep Moving Forward — 83

About the Author — 96

Acknowledgments — 97

Thanks for reading!   100

Destined for Greater Things   101

Chapter One

Obedience and Opposition

"Nice moves," Aunt Poppy said. Sweat was beginning to gather on her brow. Her sandy short-cropped hair glistened in the sunlight. "You must have been practicing while I was away."

She raised her short sword to guard her face and torso and backed away from me. She certainly looked less intimidating in her formal pantsuit, but the shirt still strained from her hulking arm muscles.

"Something like that," I replied. I didn't exactly have fighting clothes, as my mother didn't approve of this hobby. But my old, beat-up riding clothes worked well enough. "Or you're just getting old."

I took a deep breath and flung my head to toss my dark black ponytail around to my back. I rushed towards her, and she swiped her blade in my direction. At the last moment, I dropped into a crouch and swung my leg around to trip her. She jumped before I could make contact and flipped forward over my head. She lowered the edge of her short sword to my throat as autumn leaves fell around us.

"Got me again," I laughed as she pulled her sword away and offered me her hand. I happily took it and pulled myself up. The garden of the Autumn Maiden's estate wasn't meant for this sort of training, but it was always my favorite use of the grounds.

"You truly are getting better," she repeated.

I pushed some loose hair behind my ear and smirked. "Still not good enough to beat you."

"Please, girl, I have been adventuring for over a century now. You are barely within your second decade," Aunt Poppy reassured.

"I just really wanted to beat you before .... Well, you know," I admitted.

"Asha," she began sympathetically, "just because you're getting married doesn't mean you need to stop sparring with me."

"The future Autumn Maiden doesn't concern herself with the martial arts," I said, pointing a crooked finger at her, mimicking my grandmother. I pushed my nose out and opened my eyes a bit wider.

Aunt Poppy laughed. "You better not let her catch you doing that. That woman never forgets. You can trust me on that."

That causes a chill to run down my back, remembering all the times my grandmother had scolded me. It's not what she says so much as how she says it. That tone will stick with you.

"But it's more than that, Aunt Poppy. I don't want sparring to just be a womanly dalliance for me. I want to be an adventurer. I want to be like you!" I exclaimed. I meant it. The princess life never seemed to fit for me.

"I know," she said in a consolatory tone. "But sometimes we just don't get to choose our path in life."

I liked to believe she truly felt things could be different. Why else would she send me such detailed letters of her adventures all the time? I hoped she might know about a loophole to get me out of this.

"But you did!"

Aunt Poppy sighed. There were some things, it seemed, even great adventurers can't do. "That's the blessing of being the second born. I assure you, your father has made sacrifices because of his duty to the family. That is just something first borns get saddled with."

"It's not fair," I whined. I sounded like a small child. I always made sure to take advantage of my time with my aunt to get in all my overly dramatic complaints that I couldn't do in front of the rest of my family.

"That it is not, Asha. Life rarely is," Poppy said solemnly, turning to look towards the Autumn Maiden's expansive manor house.

"It's just," I began, "The way you talk about the material realm makes it sound like there is so much more opportunity there."

"It is that," Aunt Poppy admitted, "but there are troubles there too. I'll be heading back there after tonight's dinner. Perhaps if you make a good impression, your grandmother might let you tag along."

I smiled at the thought, even though I knew it was a far-fetched fantasy.

"Asha! Sister! It is almost time!" My sister Tinsley called, running out of the large decorative glass double doors on the back of the manor house.

"Very well, Tinsley," I relented and began following behind her.

"Eh, not so fast," Aunt Poppy said.

I looked down and noticed the training sword still in my hand. I handed it over.

"I get it," Aunt Poppy began, "I've had more than a few first dates that I'd wished I'd brought a weapon along, but it may not offer a good first impression."

"Probably not," I laughed.

"Hurry up, Asha!" Tinsley protested, looking back. She had already gotten prepared for the dinner with a lace-trimmed flowy yellow dress. Her black hair was tied up in an elaborate braid. "Lord Kingsley could be here any minute!"

"Tinsley," I said, running to catch up to her, "The letter said that Lord Kingsley would arrive at sundown. We have nearly two hours left."

"Yes, but he could be early. Just imagine if he comes early and you're still dirty from sparring. What would he think of our family," Tinsley worried. I could see her wringing her hands.

"Dear sister," I said, stepping in front of her, "Then surely he must know if he inconveniences us by coming early, it is my prerogative to make him wait."

I booped her nose and skipped ahead, pushing through the door to our family sitting room. I was greeted with solemn faces from my mother and grandmother.

"Take those dirty boots off this instant!" My grandmother, Arabella Alistar, screamed at me. I quickly complied and stood at near attention.

I don't know if she had already prepared for the dinner or not, as she is always dressed formally. Even though we are in our private home, she always says that the Autumn Maiden must be ready to take guests at a moment's notice. This afternoon, she was wearing a deep maroon gown with leaves embroidered around the trim. It was always leaves with her. Her gray hair was plaited in her signature three-strand braid.

"Honestly, Asha, do you have any idea how hard your mother and I have worked to ensure this house is perfect for your future husband?" Grandmother asked.

I could see my mother, Priya Mehmet Alistar, roll her deep brown eyes behind my grandmother's back. We all knew my mother had really done all the cleaning. My grandmother had only bossed her around. However, we also all knew never to question my grandmother to her face.

"Of course, grandmother. I'm so very sorry, I wasn't thinking," I replied.

"As though that is anything new. I suppose we can't ask a leopard to change its spots, can we? Priya, dear, do you think you could do something about your daughter? Please clean her up and find something appropriate for her to wear. Surely even you can manage that," my grandmother stated, waving me and my mother away.

My mother stood up and crossed the room to ascend the stairs. I lowered my head and quickly followed behind, hoping to avoid notice. I wasn't so lucky.

"Posture, Asha," my grandmother yelled, "You are going to develop a hunchback!"

"Yes, grandmother," I said sheepishly.

As we reached the upstairs hallway, I strapped myself in for the guilt trip I knew my mother was about to take me on.

"Asha Anvi Alistar," my mother almost always begins these speeches with my full name. "How can you be so careless? Don't you realize the sacrifices I've made for you? When I left Kapoor and transported my life to the Fey Realm, I left everyone I loved behind. Do you have any idea how hard that was for me!?"

"I feel like I have some idea, but I'm sure you'll tell me again," I joked, trying to lighten the mood.

"This is all some joke to you, isn't it? I don't think you realize how hard life is on the material plane. People like us are persecuted. People hate Elves," she explained.

"Mom, people hate us here! We are basically the only people in the Fey Realm with dark skin. People look at us like we are some kind of alien, which I guess, we kind of are," I argued.

"Which is why it was so incredible that your father chose to marry me. He took a risk that has the potential to elevate River Elves to levels unseen in centuries. But that can only happen if our family can move through their social customs."

"I know that, mom, but what about our customs? I don't even know all the names of our people's holidays."

"I know this is hard for you to understand, but the great hope of the River Elves rests on your shoulders. We can't make any mistakes. You can't make any mistakes. Please, listen to what I'm saying. I'm begging you," my mother pleaded.

"Very well, mother," I said, code switching back to the High Elven woman my mother wanted me to be. It often felt like the only person that saw me for me was my Aunt Poppy. It gets exhausting pretending to be someone else.

"That's good, Asha," my mother said, "Let's clean you up and make you look like a woman this Lord Kingsley would want to marry."

"Yes, mother," I relented. This wasn't an argument I was going to win.

My mother instructed me to undress as she prepared a hot bath for me. As I stood naked and alone in my bedchambers, I couldn't help but notice all the ways I could escape this place. I didn't have anything resembling a plan, but the thought of "away" sounded very appealing. The large window led to a rose garden below, just one story down. I could easily fashion a rope out of my opulent sheets and scurry my way down before my mother returned. There were no windows on the lower level directly below this room, so it wouldn't be hard to avoid detection. I'd be free to chase the life of adventure I'd always dreamed of. Though, I suppose the gardening staff may spot me and tell my family.

There's also the secret passage behind my wardrobe that leads to a dank chamber below the Autumn Manor. It is ancient and likely used by earlier generations to sneak out. It seriously made me wonder what sort of trouble my grandmother could have possibly gotten into in her youth. That wouldn't work, though; the servants now use it to travel unnoticed throughout the manor. Surely, I would be recognized.

I also briefly considered the washroom I shared with my sister, Tinsley. Tinsley was certainly downstairs with our grandmother, and I could likely sneak out there and find a way out through the back entrance of the manor. But surely someone would catch me. There were likely servants using fire magic to warm up my bath as I stood here.

Before I could earnestly consider an escape plan, my mother returned with a large, poofy, bright orange dress. There were leaf accents stitched along each seam and garish, brightly colored apples and oranges generously placed along the lengthy skirt. I'm certain many girls would find it beautiful. I found it excessive.

"What are you doing just standing in your room in the nude?" My mother chastised. "Get yourself into the bath. I'm going to have to hold your hand through every part of this if I expect it to go well."

I nodded and walked into the washroom. As promised, my mother followed, guided me into the tub, and started scrubbing my body. To this day, I can think of no act more mortifying than being an able-bodied woman, 23 years of age, while your mother bathes you like a child. I still have nightmares about it.

After my bath, my mother dressed me in the ridiculous dress she'd brought, curled my hair into luscious waves, and finished the look with a wreath of Autumn flowers atop my head. I'm sure I was the perfect image of future royalty.

By this time, I could see the sun beginning to set. My entire family had already gathered outside, awaiting Lord Kingsley's carriage. My mother and I walked out to join them. Just as we'd joined our family, a pair of alaricorns began drifting slowly into our front garden as if on cue. They were beautiful, with perfectly white manes and broad, angelic wings. Their horns shone like the finest silver and occasionally produced a subtle spark. Behind them, an elegant carriage was attached. It had gold accents and more in-laid aquamarine gemstones than were aesthetically pleasing. Aquamarine is the official gemstone of the Windsor family, and I suppose Lord Kingsley's family didn't want us thinking it was just some commoner's carriage pulled by two of the rarest steeds in all of the fey realm.

My five-year-old brother, Brigsby, was immediately enamored with the creatures.

"Those unicorns have wings!" He exclaimed to my father, the Crown Prince of Autumn, Sterling Alistar.

"They do!" He agreed. My father always understood there was no need to ruin the fun of children with semantics.

"Can I pet them?" Brigsby asked.

"We'll have to ask Lord Kingsley," my father informed. "Do you think you can wait a few moments until we introduce ourselves?"

"Yes, I can do it!" Brigsby assured.

I smiled at his youthful zeal.

As the carriage settled, the doors magically swung open, and Lord Kingsley stepped out. He was very handsome, in an objective sense. A tall elven man with a strong jawline. He had short, but flowing locks of dark brown hair. His face was cleanly shaven and completely devoid of expression. I've never understood why rich people think showing no emotion makes them more attractive. And in my experience, this isn't just an elven thing. All types of rich people think that emotion makes them ugly. To me, it makes them look bored. Knowing my young self, I'm certain I shared the same look, but only because I was actually bored. He approached my grandmother first.

"It is such an honor to meet the exalted Autumn Maiden," Lord Kingsley said as he bowed deeply.

"You may rise. We are pleased your family has elected for you to join us this evening. We hope you will enjoy the dinner we have prepared for you," my grandmother concluded, leading us into the dining hall.

"A meal prepared by the Autumn Maiden herself must be incredible," Lord Kingsley said, knowing full well that a woman of my grandmother's stature would never sully herself by preparing her own food.

My grandmother blushed and said, "The gentleman flatters."

We all lined up at the front of the dining hall as my grandmother took her seat at the front of the table.

"Asha Alistar, allow me to introduce you to Lord Kingsley Windsor, your betrothed," my grandmother said, gesturing for us to greet each other.

I wanted to make a quip about how I was with her outside when he introduced himself, but I'd already gotten myself into enough trouble. Instead, I simply said, "A pleasure," and offered him my hand.

He kissed it and said, "The pleasure is all mine. My family did not do you justice. They told me you were beautiful, but they didn't tell me you were stunning."

He was really going all out with these compliments. I giggled to avoid retching right there on the fine carpeting and retreated to my seat beside my grandmother.

He claimed his seat opposite me. And so it went with my grandmother giving each of my family permission to sit. Next, my parents, then my aunt, then finally my siblings. For once, I missed sitting with the children. At least they would be permitted to have an enjoyable conversation.

As we began eating our first course, the conversation went about as you'd expect. We spoke nothing of substance and basically kept repeating the same two or three greetings to one another. My grandmother was too intimidating for Lord Kingsley to show any vulnerability in front of... so we just talked about nothing. I grew tired of it by my third butternut squash crostini.

I excused myself and snuck into the sitting room. It was less for the leaf-patterned velvet sofas and more for the lack of immediate visual reminders of what was to come. I began pacing back and forth and considered what kind of life I would have with Lord Kingsley. One thing was for sure; it would be extraordinarily ordinary. That wasn't the life I wanted for myself. I wanted adventure, I wanted excitement and that tall glass of elven milk could not providing that for me.

"Lady Asha," I heard a male voice call from the side hallway.

I turned around and saw Lord White Bread himself.

"Hello, Lord Kingsley. I'm sorry to keep you waiting," I apologized.

"No, no trouble," he assured. "I just wanted to see if what was bothering you is the same thing that is bothering me."

This was intriguing.

"Which is?" I inquired.

"I hate these arranged marriages play act things we have to do. I hate the idea of an arranged marriage. My parents did it, and they seem happy, but I just don't know," Lord Kingsley confided.

It was nice to know I wasn't the only noble that felt frustrated with the expectation to do things just because it was what everyone had always done. Maybe we didn't have to do this. We wouldn't be the first to stray from tradition.

"My parents didn't have an arranged marriage," I confessed with a smile.

"Really?" He said with a smirk, "The Autumn Maiden's son married a woman of his choosing?"

"Turns out, this part of the fey realm doesn't have people with brown skin," I remarked.

"I had noticed that," he joked.

"I'm sorry, I don't want this life," I admitted. "I want a life of adventure, and being the future Autumn Maiden doesn't offer that to me."

"You know you'd be giving up your position as heir of one of the number two ruling families in the fey realm?" he asked.

"I do, in fact," I said. "I just don't see the appeal of mediating feuds between noble families and doing whatever the Winter Queen tells me to do."

"It does not sound like adventure, I will admit that," Lord Kingsley said.

"I don't know what to do," I said. "I don't want to trap you into this life if you don't want it."

"Oh, I want it," Lord Kingsley said, "The power and security is appealing to me. But I don't want you to feel obligated to provide that to me."

"Really?" I asked.

"Yes. You should go. Take one of my alaricorns out front and give her this," he placed a small green berry in my hand.

"What is it?" I asked.

"That is a sacred berry of the Spring Court called a Wanta. My family raises them. When fed to an alaricorn, they transport themselves and their rider to the material plane," he explained.

"Why do you think I want to go to the Material Plane?" I asked.

"Because if you run, nowhere in the Fey Realm will be safe for you. If you want adventure, that is where you'll have to go," he said.

"You're not wrong," I agreed. "How can I repay you?"

"Live the life you want," he said, "That's what I'm going to try to do."

"Thank you," I said, then I leaned in and kissed him on the lips gently. As far as first kisses go, this one certainly could have been worse.

"You're welcome, Asha Alistar," Lord Kingsley said.

"Goodbye," I said, walking quietly outside. The sensible part of me wanted to go upstairs and pack, but the adventurous side had waited too long for an opportunity like this.

As I passed through the door, I spotted my sheathed training sword leaning against the outside wall attached to a belt. I picked it up and strapped the belt around my dress.

I proceeded to approach one of the alaricorns and reached to scratch its nose. It lowered its head and happily complied. I walked around, released the carriage hitch, and mounted the alaricorn. I stroked its mane heartily and reached around to feed it the berry. As I sat astride the alaricorn, we were off. I watched the manor I had spent the entirety of my life up to that point fade from view. With a bright flash from the alaricorn's horn, we found ourselves in an open field.

I didn't have time to think about how the rest of the dinner went or what my grandmother would think when she found out, because the path to adventure lay before me. And adventure waits for no one.

Chapter Two

Out of the Fey Realm

My family home began to fade before my eyes, replaced with a bright, white light. I blinked my eyes to attempt to readjust to my new setting. It was pointless because the light was quickly overtaken by the interior of a tavern emerging into existence around me.

I barely had time to look around when I heard a man yell at me. "You've got to be kidding me!"

The tavern looked downright dingy to me, but my only frame of reference was the homes of lords and royalty. The floor was patchy hardwood, with tables and stools scattered about and varied levels of food waste distributed about the room.

The man continued, "This is the third time this month! You wizards have to stop teleporting wherever the hell you want. Some of us are trying to run an honest business around here."

He was a short man with a bit of a potbelly. He had short salt-and-pepper hair and pale skin. A bit of stubble was poking out of his face. Not entirely unappealing, if I'm being honest. Though, his ears did startle me. They were so short, only just level with his eyes. Not only that, but they were rounded. I had never seen anything like it. He wore dark clothing and an apron not unlike what I had seen my servants wear.

"And if you are not the most interesting man I have ever seen before," I exclaimed at him.

His eyes narrowed in offense. "What? You are not going to come in here and just make fun of me. What is wrong with you?"

"I'm being serious, those little ears, the two-toned hair, and the way your stomach puffs out at the front and sides. You're lovely!" I explained.

"Now, I know you're making fun of me. Wait, what did you say about my ears?" It was as though he had only just decided to look at me. I saw his eyes drift to my face, and then his face twisted into an expression of absolute horror. "You're an Elf! You can't be here!"

He moved towards the alaricorn tentatively and tried to shoo it out.

"I'm sorry, I don't know what you're saying. I mean, yes, I'm an Elf, but why is that a problem?" I asked. I legitimately had no idea what he was talking about.

"Are you being serious right now? You people were all over Anglachel when I was a kid, and we all know that you were enslaving the tribes to the west. There was even talk you people were using charm magic to take advantage of the civilized people in the city. Just because you all left doesn't mean we've forgiven you." He ranted.

Obviously, I had learned in my private princess lessons that the material realm had been colonized by my ancestors. But for the life of me, I could not understand what he was so worked up about if all this happened back when he was a kid.

"Seriously? Can't we just let bygones be bygones? When you were a kid had to be, what, about 500 years ago?" I said, gauging his age based on the people his age I had met in the Fey Realm.

I saw his facial expression shift from confusion to curiosity to rage. "What is wrong with you!?! That's such an insane thing to say, I don't even know if it's offensive. I'm only forty years old. What kind of a person lives for 500 years?"

When I tell you I was confused, that doesn't begin to describe it. What kind of a world had I teleported to? I know I've lived a sheltered life, but surely not this sheltered.

"I'm afraid I don't have the slightest idea what you're talking about," I concluded.

The man's countenance shifted back to confusion. At least now, we felt the same way about the situation.

"Are you trying to tell me that you've never met a Human before?" He asked.

"I'm trying to tell you that I've never even heard that word before. What did you say? Humis?" I asked. Was he talking about a kind of animal?

"HU-MAN," he pronounced exaggeratedly. "I'm talking about most of the people that live in this city."

"Please, I'm not a child. Don't talk to me like one. But I suppose, yes, you are the first of these Human creatures I've met. That explains why you are so unique," I reasoned.

"I assure you, I'm painfully average," he explained. "But you still can't be here. Your people still aren't exactly loved in these parts. Why are you here?"

"I'm looking for adventure," I answered sincerely. "I'm running away from an arranged marriage."

"That does sound bad," he said in a neutral tone that didn't really express sympathy. "I wish there was something I could do for you."

"Maybe there is," I said brightly. "Would you like to purchase this alaricorn?"

I would need money if I was going to live here. Selling this creature that isn't even mine seemed to make the most sense.

"Is that what that unicorn with wings is called?" He asked.

"And you thought I was ridiculous for not knowing what Humans were," I laughed. He did not seem amused.

"I could take it off your hands," he replied. "How about one gold?"

I didn't know anything about the currency of this world, but I could tell when someone was trying to screw me over.

"No, thank you," I said, nudging the alaricorn forward with my heel.

He ran in front of me.

"Come on," he said. "What about three gold?"

"I'm fine," I continued. "You should get out of the way. You may think unicorns are nice, but alaricorns can be straight-up vicious."

I didn't actually know if either of those statements were true, but it sounded good.

"Fine then, leave. See if I care," He screamed at me. Suddenly, he was upset that I wanted to leave. These Humans must be fickle creatures.

The alaricorn walked up to the door, and it was still closed. I didn't know how to do this without getting down, but I didn't want to face the tavern owner. I tried to nudge the alaricorn forward again. It lowered its head, and a beam of magic shot out of its horn and disintegrated the door.

That was unexpected. Perhaps they *were* vicious. Maybe I should consider keeping it.

The alaricorn pushed onto the busy street and began to push through the crowd.

Anglachel was an enormous city. I had gone to the Fey Court with my grandmother, and while impressive, it was nothing like this! The alaricorn I was riding was surrounded by people on either side. There was some sort of outdoor market on either side of the road selling all sorts of various products. I thought about jumping down and trying to get something to eat, the smells filling the air were so unusual compared to the infinite autumnal cuisine I was used to, but I still had no money. I also couldn't help but notice all of the eyes glaring up at me. Like the tavern owner, I think they were looking at my ears.

There was a wreath of autumn flowers atop my head like a crown. I took it off and worked the weaving to make it bigger. I also fluffed up the flowers a little bit. Finally, I placed it back on my head, but now it was wide enough to cover my most prominent elven feature. I didn't want to deceive anyone, but I also wasn't trying to get killed on my first day here.

I didn't know where this crowd was taking me. Everyone appeared to be moving with purpose to their own individual places, yet they were all moving as a unit through this market. People were stopping at the stalls along the edges, but most of the masses were pushing in the same direction.

I didn't love this. I had run away from the Fey Realm because I didn't have any control over where my life was going. This was all a little too literal for my tastes.

I noticed an ornate-looking sidewalk heading to the right that was far less populated. I careened the alaricorn in that direction and peeled off of the crowd. After traveling past a series of buildings, I was surprised to be greeted with a large green space. There was a sprawling sea of grass on either side of this sidewalk. I saw people that appeared to be around my age throwing balls back and forth, laying on blankets while reading books, and doing group dances together. W

I heard someone mention something about classes, and I realized I was on the grounds of a school. I went to a private school in the Fey Realm, all about being the perfect elven noble. It was nothing like this. These people looked free. This was the independence that I'd come here for.

As I contemplated this, I heard a high-pitched feminine voice directed at me.

"Is your alaricorn friendly?" A petite blonde girl said.

If I thought the tavern owner was cute, then this girl was downright adorable. Her skin was as light and pinkish as a newborn baby. Her hair was straight and long, and her eyes shone a stunning blue. She was smiling, displaying her slightly buck teeth. She wore a fringed leather jacket over a plaid button-up shirt. The bottom of her shirt was tucked into a straight pink shirt that went all the way down to her boots. I thought she was stunning. Is this what love feels like?

"I'm sorry, I asked if your alaricorn was friendly. I'd like to pet it," the girl repeated. I hadn't responded because I'd been too busy staring at her.

"Actually, I don't know," I replied. "We'd only met a few hours ago."

I saw her darling face scrunch up in thought. Could she get any cuter?

"Only one way to find out," she said. I took note of her adventurous spirit, maybe I could talk her into joining me. She slowly reached her hand to the alaricorn's long mane. It leaned its head into her hand as she gave it some scratches.

Apparently, it was friendly. Good to know.

The girl looked up at me with those big blue eyes and smiled.

"I'm Traci," she said. "Pleased to meet you both."

"I'm Asha," I said. "You're the first person I've had a pleasant interaction with since I've gotten here. Nice to meet you too."

"That's strange," she said, scrunching up her face again. "Everyone at Arcana University is usually really welcoming. What are you here for?"

"That's a complicated question," I began.

"Then why don't we go somewhere more comfortable? I can teleport us to my dorm room so you can feel free to say whatever you want," she offered.

I know that many people would say it is irresponsible to go to a second location with a stranger I'd just met, but those people have never been royals. I had gotten so used to following the person with the most authoritative voice in the room for so long, it felt almost instinctual to go with her. That, and I didn't hate the idea of being in a room alone with the cutest girl I had ever seen in my life.

I tried to summon my most even response. "If you think that would be appropriate."

"Sure it is. Everyone hangs out at each others' dorms around here," she explained.

"Then let's teleport."

She lifted her free hand up to my leg.

"May I?" she asked.

"Of course," I said, maybe a little too eagerly. It's hard to explain, but there's something about abandoning an arranged marriage that makes you want to jump into the first potential relationship you can choose yourself.

She placed her hand on my leg, and I felt magical energy surround my body. Before I had time to process what was happening, we were already outside a different building.

"That was fast," I noted.

"Sure, teleportation is kinda my thing," she bragged. "Why don't we leave your alaricorn at the stables here? I can use my student ID to check it in."

I agreed, and I followed along as she completed the paperwork. There was something nice about the familiarity of being told what to do. Clearly, this place was some sort of school for higher learning. Elves are always constant learners, but we usually have private tutors after we come of age. Apparently, these Humans had a school for those who had just come of age. It sounded fun, but I had to remind myself that I came here for adventure, not school.

I learned through context that Arcana University was a magic school that taught magic users how to tap into the different disciplines. I'd always found my magic classes dreadfully boring, so that did help to assuage my burgeoning interest.

Traci led us a few flights up a stairway and down a hallway. We stopped at a pretty nondescript door, where she pulled out a key and pushed it open.

The door may have been nondescript, but this room was not. Traci apparently had a room to herself, and it was covered in pink and posters of various breeds of horse, unicorn, pegasus, and alaricorn. I would later discover that Traci is what Humans colloquially call a "horse girl." I actually found this charming. There was something nice about categorizing people by their interests rather than their race or status.

Traci jumped on her bed and gestured to a fuzzy, foldable pink chair across from it. I took her cue and fell into it.

"So, what brought you here, Asha?" Traci asked.

"I'm looking for adventure," I said bluntly, like a child that was asked what they wanted to be when they grew up. That might be because Traci was the first person to actually ask me what I wanted.

"That's what a lot of people here say," she said. "Looks like you found yourself in the right place. Your clothes look lovely, but would you want to change into something a little more comfortable? I have stuff in the closet."

"I'm good for now," I said. I wanted to see just how much I could trust this girl before I dropped my guard around her.

"At least take off that flower crown. It looks really uncomfortable. It's pressing against your ears," she said with a tinge of concern.

"Do you promise you won't tell anyone?" I asked her. I remembered how we got up here, so I could run if I needed to.

"Sure," she said, puzzled.

I carefully removed the flower crown and let my long, pointed ears out.

Traci released an audible gasp. "You're an Elf."

"That I am," I responded.

"Are you going to control me? I heard that Elves do that. My parents told me," she said, clearly petrified and talking a little too fast.

"Goodness, no. What is wrong with all of you people?" I answered. "I came here for adventure. Do you really think all Elves want is to enslave and control people?"

"Honestly," Traci paused. "Yes? Elves basically controlled this realm until just before I was born. This is all pretty fresh for all of us."

Suddenly, every reaction I received since arriving made much more sense. I knew that my people had their hands in a lot of different realms, but I didn't know we went around conquering them. Clearly, I was much more sheltered than I had realized. And my people did not teach us the entirety of our history. I had learned about the great artists and magical discoveries in elven culture, but I knew nothing about our past as tyrants.

I was more than a little shellshocked. "I didn't know that."

"Wow, you must be really confused," Traci laughed.

I appreciated her bringing levity to the situation.

"You have no idea."

"Well, Arcana University was actually built to commemorate the Elves leaving this realm. The Elves taught Humans magic, but always kept people at arm's length. The school opened to keep magical knowledge alive," Traci explained.

"You know a lot," I said.

"Just what every Human learns in school. I'm just badly parroting what my history teacher taught me when I was little," she said modestly.

"So you're learning magic?" I asked.

"I'm trying. My spatial magic is an innate ability I was born with. I can teleport anywhere. But learning new spells has been a challenge. I *hate* memorizing!"

"That sounds bad," I agreed. I got through all of my school years by breezing through with my family's name. I couldn't imagine actually doing schoolwork.

"Yeah, magic school hasn't been what I'd imagined," she confided.

"Then come with me! We can adventure together," I offered. Having someone that actually understood this world traveling with me would make all of this a whole lot easier. And if she wanted to explore our burgeoning relationship further, who am I to object?

"I can't. My parents paid my tuition. I have to finish the year out." She looked disappointed. I had her on the hook, I just had to reel her in.

"Why? You just said it sucks. And you can't tell me you wouldn't love to travel with that unicorn," I tempted. Light manipulation felt appropriate in this situation.

"Alaricorn," she quickly corrected. "But I really would!"

"Let's do it! You and me! We can take on all of... what is this world called again?" I asked, interrupting my dramatic rallying cry.

"Galevyn," Traci said.

"We can take on all of Galevyn!" I finished.

"Yeah," she said, slightly more confident now. "I can be an adventurer!"

I was sure she wouldn't blame me for this rash decision. She wouldn't agree to go with me if she didn't already want to. Logistics be damned, we were riding a high here.

"Yes, we are adventurers," I said. I couldn't believe this was really happening.

Chapter Three

A Life of Adventure

"I just wish we didn't have to split up," Traci complained lovingly, looking at me with those big, blue eyes. It had been three months since I arrived in Galevyn, and Traci and I had become more than just friends that went on adventures together.

"I know, Trace, but I need to stay near Maxwell, and you need to keep a lookout for anything suspicious," I explained the plan to her again.

"O.K., just take care of yourself. I won't be here to save you," she teased.

"We both know that I'll be the one to do the saving," I retorted.

"Asha, we're in this together. We save each other," she repeated. This was one of our regular refrains.

"You're right. I know you're right. We save each other," I said. I embraced her one last time before she got into position. We gave each other a quick goodbye kiss. Traci teleported away.

Since running away from my arranged marriage and traveling to Galevyn to become an adventurer, I was surprised to find out that there was so much adventuring in the city of Anglachel. Anglachel is a massive city, and there is no shortage of businesses needing help getting rid of rodents, students needing help finding specific herbs from the Jungle of Despair, and packages that nobles wanted picked up. This wasn't exactly what I imagined a life of adventure would look like, but it was a nice change of pace from all of the ball gowns and etiquette classes.

Speaking of ball gowns, I was also surprised at how much coin I was able to get out of the one I was wearing when I came here. As long as I kept my Elf ears hidden, the nobles in this city were absolutely fascinated with the elven culture. You'd almost think the Elves weren't mind controlling most of them just 20ish years ago. Traci and I were able to use the money from the dress to outfit ourselves in adventuring gear. She traded her "horse girl" clothes for something more practical. She now wears a Human-created fabric called denim for her pants, and thank the gods, she found a way to add the cute leather fringes to those. I bought a navy blue cloak with a hood to make it easier to cover my ears. I also managed to find leather armor that had been dyed white. It really complemented the cloak and looked pretty cute. I loved it when I didn't have to sacrifice fashion for function.

The job we found ourselves in right now has been pretty interesting. A local politician had contracted us to protect him during his rallies. His name is Maxwell Canterly, and his campaign was challenging the relatively recent status quo of Anglachel. As it stood, the nobles basically ran things, and the government only really served the nobles. Canterly thought that the government should be lifting up the poorest instead of keeping them down. He said the quiet part out loud, and his competitors hated him for calling them out. Because of this boldness, he was worried that the political establishment would be coming for him. Thus far, it has been a pretty easy gig. Traci and I would stand guard, and no one really tried anything. I guess politics hasn't had time to get corrupt here yet.

I especially appreciated this job because it caught me up on Anglachelian current events. I was utterly clueless when I'd first gotten here, and Traci can only explain so much before she starts to get tired of the questions. Not to mention, this whole romantic relationship thing was a trip! Who knew having actual feelings for a person, and the physical perks that came along with it, could improve your mood so much?

I trusted that Maxwell Canterly was a progressive person who wanted to help the lower classes, and Traci seemed to agree, but truthfully– I was here for the pay. He could have been absolutely vile as long as the coin was good. I will admit he seemed sincere enough in his speeches, and the crowds sure seemed to love him. After growing up as one of the few colorful ones in an otherwise lily-white family, it was uplifting to see so many different species of people together. His platform to expand voting rights to all citizens has rallied not just progressive Human nobles; but also the Halflings, Gnomes, Mascaras, and Dwarves. It was hard not to get caught up in the excitement.

I spotted Traci on top of a roof on the other side of the crowd. She would handle any threats that entered from that side. I was hidden by the stairs leading up to the stage. My job was to protect Canterly at all costs. I hadn't quite determined where my limit for "all" was yet, so I kept agreeing with him. Hopefully, it would never get that close. I began scanning the crowd, nearby alleys, and rooftops for any direct threats to Canterly. So far, so good. As he began speaking, I kept scanning but allowed myself to tune into what he was saying.

"People of Angalchel, the revolution is not yet over!" He screamed into the crowd to uproarious applause. "The parliament thinks that their work is done. The Elves have left, and the charmed enslaved folks have been freed, but I think we all know that's not enough! Yes, Queen Florence and her lackeys were generous enough to allow the formerly enslaved to keep their shabby servants' quarters that their ancestors built in the first place. Meanwhile, she lives in her castle's lap of luxury, and the parliament's members serve from their lavish manors. I'll be the first to admit that I, too, grew up as a noble. But my eyes have been opened to the struggles of the majority of Anglachelians. It is time to accept that the government needs to be built by more than wealthy Human nobles. It must be built by all of the people of Anglachel!"

The crowd once again erupted in applause. I managed to see the twinkle of metal emerging from a nearby rooftop. I leapt onto the stage and rushed to the side near the crowd. The crossbow bolt sped directly toward Canterly, and it would have hit its target if I had been just a bit slower. I pulled my aunt's sword free from its scabbard and knocked the arrow away from Canterly, in the opposite direction from the crowd. I spotted a shadowy figure shifting away from the rooftop the bolt had emerged from. I sheathed my sword and raced atop

the roof. I craved adventure, and a roof chase was just
what the physician ordered.

The rooftops of Anglachel are one of the few places
in the city I can feel at home. The buildings here are
clearly of elven design, and standing on top of the roofs
reminds me of the late nights I would look out the
window of my bedroom tower and imagine a life away
from all the royal nonsense that became my day-to-day.
It was not unusual for me to climb over my balcony
and jump to the other buildings in the castle to listen in
on grown-up conversations. I didn't care much about
what my family members were talking about, but I en-
joyed the thrill of knowing things I wasn't supposed
to. This childhood pastime was one of the few skills
from my old life that carried over to this new one as
an adventurer. Chasing after marks on rooftops wasn't
a common practice, but it did seem to happen often
enough.

The cloaked figure that had shot at Canterly was
about three buildings away from me. The figure was
short and, while nimble, seemed to have trouble reach-
ing the speeds my longer Elf limbs could. The figure
was throwing a grappling hook across the way so they
could swing over to the next building. I knew this was
my chance. I pulled a dagger from under my cloak and
threw it at the rope. It didn't carve straight through the

rope. Apparently, that kind of thing is really hard to do, but it *did* knick it on one side. It frayed the rope enough that it would at least make it a precarious leap for the figure. I raced across the rooftops between us to close the gap.

The figure looked back apprehensively as I moved closer. He appeared to be a masculine-looking Halfling. He considered his options and decided to take the risk of the rope. He leaped off the rooftop, and I cringed a bit as I saw the rope unravel a bit at the cut. It didn't snap, but it did stretch long enough to alter his course. Instead of landing on the adjacent building, he dangled over the edge. I saw him quickly scurrying up the rope, but I was faster. I leaped across the gap and landed on the rooftop, my feet on either side of the rope. I drew my sword and waited for the Halfling to make his way up.

I saw one set of fingertips grasp the edge of the rooftop, but the other streaked over the edge and threw a dagger in my general direction. Admittedly, I should have seen it coming. What can I say? This adventurer life is new for me. I managed to slide away from most of it, but it did slice a neat slit across my bicep. The dagger clambered to the roof after hitting the back of my cloak. I knew it had to of punctured a hole in it.

"You asshole! This cloak is new!" I screamed at the Halfling.

He sprang around the wall and landed, facing me on the rooftop. He had another dagger drawn by the time he landed. This guy was pretty good.

"Yeah, and my plan wasn't, but you ruined it. So, I guess we're even," he spat. He gritted his teeth, ready for a fight.

I really didn't want to have to fight this guy, but I was also excited for my first real scuffle as an adventurer. I took a defensive stance. He charged toward me, and I caught his dagger with my sword. I used his momentum to spin him onto the other side of me.

"Why are you after Canterly? You know his policies would help the Halflings of this city, right?" I asked as he readied another attack. I leap-frogged over him as he attempted to plunge his dagger into me.

"He's short-sighted," the Halfling growled. "His plans help the people of the city, but what about the people outside of it?"

I was confused. "He is running to join the parliament for the city. How would his plans have anything to do with the people outside of it?" I ducked down and swept my leg to try to trip him. He saw it coming and jumped over it. He came down hard with his dagger and almost stabbed my leg, but I managed to get it away in time.

"Typical Human," he said with a level of malice I had only ever heard my grandmother use to talk about the other seasonal monarchs. "He plans to build more housing in the slums. Where is that going to go? It will have to extend into the Jungle. When Anglachel was founded, it promised the indigenous people that it would never expand further into the jungle."

He leapt back and chucked his dagger at my abdomen. I easily swatted it away with my sword. Either I was better than I thought, or he was losing his will to harm me.

"My dude," I began, "We live in a world of magic! Surely there must be some solution to build housing that doesn't encroach into the Jungle. I'm sure if you talked to him. . "

"Why would Canterly listen to me? I'm beneath him, literally and figuratively. He doesn't care what I would have to say, especially not about indigenous Anglachelians. No one seems to care about them. They always get left out of the conversation!"

The tension eased out of him a little bit. He was ready to have a conversation instead of a fight. I took advantage of it and tackled him. His body collapsed from the momentum, and I placed my foot on his chest.

Now that he wasn't a threat, the tension in my shoulders could ease a bit. "Why do you even care about the indigenous Anglachelians? Aren't they Orcs, Goblins, and Humans? You're a Halfling, right?"

"Yes, I'm a Halfling. It may surprise you that people can care about people that aren't themselves," he said. He meant it to be sarcastic, but it stung more than it should've. I couldn't help but think about all the responsibility I ran away from in the fey realm. My little sister would probably have to marry that guy. Was she ready for that kind of commitment when I knew I couldn't handle it?

"Yeah, I get that," I managed to get out, a little more strained than I would have liked.

"I grew up in the slums," he explained. "I used to sneak across the border and play in the jungle. I'm not indigenous, but I grew up with them."

"Then I'll help you. I work for Canterly; we can talk to him together," I offered. "My name is Asha. What's yours?"

"I'm The Scourge," he said in a falsely deep voice.

"You can't be serious," I laughed.

"Yes, I go by The Scourge," he repeated indignantly.

"That can't be your name. Make up a nor-mal-sounding fake name. That's better than 'The Scourge,'" I said.

"Come on, you've got me pinned to the ground. Can you at least let me have this?" He asked. He sounded more like a young Halfling this time. I appreciated him dropping his mask around me.

"O.K.," I relented. "I'll call you 'The Scourge.'"

I searched his cloak and pockets for any additional weapons and walked back to Canterly. It felt strange to complete a mission by befriending the would-be killer instead of offing him. Was I a bad adventurer? I decided it was best not to think about it.

Chapter Four

Freaks Have to Stick Together

"Why didn't you go to school here?" The Scourge asked me.

Traci and I had been working with him ever since his attempted homicide at the rally. Canterly started doing less of the big public rallies and more private events. This was probably better for his safety, but not as good for our coin pouches.

I thought back to my time in the Fey realm and crinkled my nose. "When I came here, I had already been through enough lessons to last a lifetime."

"So you already know some magic?"

"Oh, gods no," I guffawed. "I used my magic lessons to catch up on sleep."

Traci's parents had come down from North Angalchel to visit her. She met them outside of her old dorm building because she still hadn't told them that she'd dropped out of school. I wasn't with her because she still hadn't told them about me. I'm not bitter about it.

"What got you so tired, rich girl?" He teased.

"I always stayed up late reading letters from my Aunt Poppy. I had always dreamed of coming here and being an adventurer," I confessed.

"Where's here? You're not from Anglachel?" The Scourge asked. It was an innocent enough question. He couldn't have known I was a runaway princess.

"I'm just gonna say I'm not from around here. Let me have some secrets."

"Fine, fine. I'll stop asking you about your past. For now."

We'd picked up a job to liberate a forbidden scroll of divination from Arcana University. We don't usually take jobs that might enable someone evil to destroy the world or whatever, but what harm could someone do with divination? Make money betting on a land orca race? That seemed fine. But since Traci was busy misleading her parents, The Scourge and I had to do this one on our own. Which is why we're wandering around the campus disguised as students discussing my past. I wore one of Traci's old school uniforms with a purple blazer and a plaid skirt. The Scourge was wearing a black wizard's robe over his usual infiltration gear.

"Which one of these buildings is the library?" The Scourge inquired, looking from building to building.

"I think Traci said it was on the North Eastern side of campus near the lake. Or did she say it wasn't near the lake? Something like that," I answered.

"You don't sound too sure."

"What? I just told you I never went here. How am I supposed to know everything about the campus?"

"You could have asked Traci for directions. Or we could have done this when she's not busy. What's keeping her anyway?"

"I wish you'd stop asking so many questions," I snapped defensively. "Traci is busy. The posting had a time limit. We're the ones that are completing it. Do you need to know anything else?"

"It sounds like you've decided I don't," he said, sounding a little hurt.

I wasn't trying to hide anything from him, it was just. The more he knew the more he'd have to know. Traci and I decided that it was best not to let him know I was an Elf. If he knew Traci was meeting with her parents, he would wonder why I wasn't with them. If he knew that she didn't want me to meet her parents, he would think there was something going on. He's not dumb. He'd start digging around, and he wouldn't have to dig much deeper than under my hood. Or in this case, my hat. The student that I was disguised as wore a hat.

"Hey! You! Kid!" The Scourge shouted towards a passing student with long blonde hair wearing a similar uniform to mine. She stopped and looked down at him.

"Where is the library?" He demanded.

"This way, just past Meren hall," she said automatically, pointing in a North Easterly direction.

"Thanks!" I said brightly, dragging The Scourge away as the student proceeded on her way. We'd gotten lucky.

"What was that?" I said, rounding on him.

"I was figuring out where we had to go. More than you've done."

"You can be upset, but don't ruin the mission because you're mad at me. Fellow students don't usually call each other 'kid.'"

"Fine. You can do this by yourself if you want. I don't need the money that bad," The Scourge said, walking away, but still in the direction of the library.

"O.K. First of all, that's a lie. We both know you need the money. Second, I want you here. I don't understand what you're so mad about."

The Scourge stopped and turned his head towards me. "I just thought we were becoming friends. I must have been mistaken."

That took me aback. We'd worked quite a few jobs together in the past month, but I didn't realize he was looking for friends. I just thought we were work colleagues. Of course, it's not like I'm drowning in friends here. Running away to another realm and leaving behind everyone you've ever known will do that.

I walked up to him and knelt down so we'd be face-to-face. "Do you trust me?"

"Bloody hell, Asha. We've each saved each other's lives a couple times each now. What does it take for you to trust someone?"

"I was just giving you a chance to back out. This is going to be a lot."

A beat passed between us.

"Just tell me whatever you want to tell me!" The Scourge stated definitively.

I looked around to make sure no one was close to us, and I took off my hat. I watched as The Scourge's eyes widened, and he took a couple of big steps back.

"You're a- a- a," he stammered.

"Yes, I'm an Elf," I finished for him, securing my hat back in place.

We stayed there looking at each other for what felt like an eternity. I couldn't read his expression. He was clearly surprised, but that was all I got. Eventually, he laughed.

"Well, I guess that explains it. Traci can't introduce you to anyone in her life. You're a freak! Honestly, it's a little reassuring," He finished.

"A freak? Reassuring? I don't get you," I said, standing back up.

"That's my point! No one gets me! I'm a freak, too! We freaks have to stick together, that's the only way anything's going to get done."

"You don't have more questions? Why am I here? Who I really am?" I asked. This seemed too easy.

"Hells, Asha, I don't need your life story. I just wanted to know the reason why we were working this job alone. If the job becomes harder because the only person that knows where we're going can't be here, I want more than 'she's busy.'"

"That's actually fair." I was impressed at his practicality. "What do you say we grab a drink after this, and I can fill you in on a couple of those details."

"You must have one hell of a story," The Scourge rightly presumed.

"That I do, buddy. That I do."

Chapter Five

A Dragon in the Sewer

When I ditched my cushy arranged marriage to become an adventurer, I did not picture myself walking through the sewers of Anglachel. For the first time since coming to this world, the formal dinners and diplomatic trips seemed more appealing than what I was doing now. Walking through literal shit will do that to a person's perspective.

We ended up on this job a few months after The Scourge joined up with Traci and me. I couldn't tell what was harder to believe. The fact one of my former enemies had become one of my closest friends, or me liking that friend enough to actually call him something as ridiculous as "The Scourge." What can I say? The little guy grows on ya'.

After the election, political bodyguard work had pretty much dried up. That meant that we had to start doing extermination jobs again. This one actually came from the first guy I'd met upon coming to Galevyn. Thank the gods he didn't remember me after I'd changed out of my ball gown. It turns out princesses are like everyone else. His name turned out to be Kyle Stringer, and his establishment had been experiencing an infestation of slugs. He said they were mostly contained to the cellar, but one of the sticky fellers made their way onto a table every now and then, and the patrons weren't into it.

After a good hour of checking behind every barrel, crate, and shelf in the cellar, we noticed the slugs were coming out of a hole leading to a much larger chamber under the tavern. We broke through and found ourselves in the sewers of the largest city in all of Galevyn. It smelled exactly how I imagined it would. We saw a long string of slugs all headed to Stringer's place. We knew the most logical thing to do was to follow the slugs. Hence wading through Humanoid waste.

"Hey, Scourge, how much longer do you think we need to go?" I asked.

"Why the hells are you asking me?" The Scourge replied.

"I don't know. You just strike me as a guy that would go creeping around in sewers."

"That feels like an insult," The Scourge said, smiling. He knew I didn't actually mean anything by it. I shrugged in his direction to complete the bit. Traci shook her head.

"This pipe should open up in a bit. We're getting pretty close to the center of the sewer system," Traci said.

"How did you know that?" I asked.

"Even I'm a little surprised at that one," The Scourge admitted.

"At Arcana University, they would have the teleport students practice in the sewers. They'd have us memorize the maps and try to teleport to specific points without having actually been there. I've not been here before, but I've definitely been forced to memorize the map," Traci said.

"I'm impressed, babe. I'd kiss you if we didn't both look and smell like shit," I complimented.

"Thank the gods for small favors," The Scourge quipped.

"I know you love us," I said to The Scourge, ruffling his hair through his hood.

"Did you just get feces all over my cloak?" He complained.

"Maybe," I said matter-of-factly. All three of us laughed. It felt good to have people to be myself around. I take back what I said about preferring to be in an arranged marriage.

We heard a loud roar ahead. We also noticed that the sewer water was getting harder to walk through.

"What was that?" Traci asked.

"Beats me. I still don't even know all the different kinds of people here, much less the monsters," I said.

"It can't be a dragon, right?" The Scourge said skeptically. "Do you think the thicker wastewater could be a clue?"

I looked down and noticed that it was actually getting thicker. It was slushy, like it was partially frozen. I also noticed a number of slugs stuck to the wall, also frozen.

I poked at one with my dagger. It was as solid as a rock. "Ice is everywhere. Is that anything?"

"Blue dragons produce a cold aura," Traci said. "I learned about them in school."

Things either got even chillier, or I just shivered at the thought of fighting a dragon. Admittedly, it was scary, but I was actually pretty excited at the prospect of having a real challenge.

"Alright, guys," I began, "let's just accept that this is a dragon. If it's not, we'll be better prepared for whatever is there." We needed to be ready for what was ahead.

We crept forward, and the narrow pipe did open up into a large open space. Sitting in the center of the opening was a huge lizard-like creature that I could only presume was a dragon. I didn't know if we were ready for this, but I had to put on a strong front.

"We've got this, guys," I said as we prepared to fight a blue dragon.

The dragon hadn't quite noticed us yet, which gave us a quick moment to arrange ourselves strategically. We couldn't speak, as it could alert the beast, but we'd been working together long enough that we didn't need to. I spotted a great sniping location on a large pipe against the opposite wall. I pointed it out to Traci, and she silently teleported onto it. The Scourge had already slipped off, inevitably finding a hiding spot in the shadows. That left only me. I always started our fights because I was the best at getting creatures' attention. That basically meant I was the loudest. I drew my sword and took a deep breath.

"Hey, ugly, come here often?" I yelled in the dragon's general direction.

Its head snapped in my direction faster than I would have thought possible, and it began growling at me, but in a tone and canter that sounded suspiciously like a language. Hell, if I knew what it was saying, so I charged it, raising my sword. The dragon opened its mouth, exposing its toothy maw, and a blue glow sprang in my direction. I threw my shoulder in the opposite direction and rolled away, narrowly dodging the breath attack. The wet excrement immediately froze onto my white leather armor. I grimaced, thinking about what it would take to clean it after this fight. It's true that stains on armor give it more character, but I tend to prefer blotches from the blood of my enemies as opposed to sewer water and glowing phlegm.

The dragon closed its mouth and readjusted its massive body to face me. Before it could determine its next move, Traci and The Scourge fired shots into the dragon. At least they tried to. Traci's crossbow bolt scratched across the dragon's blue scales and splashed into the water below. The Scourge, however, managed to fire a bolt into the corner of the dragon's left eye. It raised its front claw to paw at its fresh injury, which was just the opportunity I was waiting for. I raced under it and quickly scanned for weaknesses. The majority of its scales were pretty airtight, but I did notice that at the joint connecting its claw to its torso, there was a slight gap while it had it raised. I ran towards the opposite claw and vertically scaled it, flipping in the direction of the exposed flesh. I stabbed upward before I began my descent, and I could feel my blade sinking into something meaty. I held tightly to my sword to ensure my body weight would be enough to pull it free from the now-tensed dragon muscle. I landed in a crouching position and rolled backwards to position myself firmly under the center of its torso.

While I was doing this, Traci had realized that sniping it wasn't going to work. She instead changed strategies and worked to guarantee The Scourge's shots did the most damage possible. She accomplished this by teleporting to an area on top of the dragon and using her spatial magic to remove individual scales from the dragon. It was still a challenge for The Scourge to hit the openings, but he was doing a pretty good job.

For all of our efforts, the dragon certainly seemed annoyed with us. However, it didn't seem to be all that hurt. There was the slightest trickle of blood coming from the wound I had caused, but like after someone gets a shot at a clinic. We were fighting like hell against this dragon, and it felt like we were poking at it. I was starting to feel like we were a little out of our depth.

The dragon began shaking like a dog after a bath, and I saw Traci fly across the room, heading towards shallow water. I sped in her direction in hopes of breaking her fall. The Scourge caught onto what I was doing and attempted to pull the dragon's attention away from me. He pulled a black powder explosive from his belt and chucked it at the dragon. He aimed his crossbow and shot a bolt at the bomb. It ignited and exploded near the dragon's flank, shifting its focus to The Scourge.

Meanwhile, I wasn't going to reach Traci in time to catch her, but I could throw my body under her to break her fall. I dove, face up, into the water, and Traci smashed into me, hard. I was sore all over, but we were both alive.

As we both crawled to our feet, we saw The Scourge wasn't so lucky. The dragon had managed to spot him and held him in its teeth. It slung The Scourge around and threw him in our general direction. I raced to break his fall the same way I had Traci's, but I could see that I was already too late. His body bounced through the muck and settled against the chamber wall. The wounds from the dragon's fangs went straight through him. There was no surviving that. I uselessly ran to his side and cradled him in my arms.

"Scourge," I screamed. " You're o.k., right? We can make it out."

Tears began streaming down my cheeks.

"We have to get out of here," Traci cried, kneeling at my side. I barely registered that she had said anything at all.

I felt her hand on my shoulder and the lifeless form of my friend faded before my eyes. I was in Kyle Stringer's basement, staring at the ground while my arms cradled nothing.

I bolted to my feet and rounded on Traci.

"What did you do?" I screamed. "You left him behind!"

My voice quivered, and I was shaking all over.

"I can only teleport two people. You know that," she said apologetically.

"But we could have helped him," I argued. "We could have brought him out and healed him."

"He was gone, Ash," Traci said, explaining something I already knew to be true. "There was nothing we could have done."

"But adventuring was supposed to be fun," I said blankly. "This was supposed to be fun."

Chapter Six

Picking Up the Pieces

It had been a long year since we'd fought that dragon. I used to think we were invincible. Now I know that's not true. At least, not for all of us. Traci and I have been together now for three years. She has been great during all of this. She was always great at taking care of people. This has brought us closer, but I don't know how I feel about it. I don't want to get close to these people if it means I could lose them at any moment. I convinced myself it was o.k. because Traci is not just "these people." She is someone that I will do whatever it takes to protect.

We continued adventuring, taking two-person jobs for a while because that was the life we lived. We didn't really have the resume to do much else. The problem; was that when you'd been doing this as long as we have, people started expecting you to do more. The regular clients didn't want to keep throwing us the easy jobs because they couldn't afford not to meet the new players. Which meant they wanted to give us more dangerous jobs because they knew we could handle them. That meant we had to start finding people to add to our team again. That meant we had to spend lots of time with people I knew we would inevitably lose.

Our recruits are friendly enough. Duri is a Halfling from Yokuatsu. She risked it all to come to Anglachel on a makeshift raft with a handful of others like her. After finding homes and jobs for all of her compatriots, she had built up an impressive network of the city's criminal underground. She leveraged that to find jobs stealing very specific things for wealthy patrons. When she met us, she was happy to put a bit of distance between herself and the city's crime lords.

Pegutsai is an Orc that lives in the Jungle. She knew The Scourge from way back, and we started to become fond of her after she helped us plan a tribal funeral for him. The Scourge always identified more with the natives than his family in the slums. It was what he would have wanted. When she heard that we'd been hired to harvest the pollen from a Luminescent Green Peony, she knew we'd need her help. It is a delicate process, which Duri or I could handle, but Pegutsai told us it was in a dangerous part of the Jungle. She said she could help us minimize the number of nasties we ran into.

I hated the idea of bringing someone I cared about on a job other than Traci. It's not so hard to protect one person, but it gets much harder when you're trying to protect everyone. I knew I'd end up having to choose, and I was going to choose Traci. It didn't seem fair to bring Pegutsai along without her knowing that. But she was always really perceptive. There's a good chance she already had an idea of what she was walking into.

In the Fey Realm, whenever my mother lost someone from her side of the family, she commissioned a painting of them. She knew she couldn't abandon her position in the Autumn Court to go home to mourn, but she did what she could from the castle. She would display the painting prominently in the family room and hang a wreath of flowers around it. She would leave it up for ten days, placing a fresh wreath of flowers each day. My grandmother hated it because it constantly reminded her that her son had married a River Elf. My mother would do it for relatives she had never met. I think it was her way of silently protesting my grandmother's blatant racism.

I picked up a bouquet of fresh flowers from the market. Traci and I couldn't afford to have a painting commissioned of The Scourge, but luckily I have always been pretty artistic. I had sketched a number of drawings of him whenever he was alive. I removed the old flowers from around the sketch and fashioned a new wreath with the flowers from the market. Ever since The Scourge died, I'd begun a tradition of thinking about him before every job. Traci has told me that it seems excessive and that a year is too long to actively mourn, but I couldn't let myself forget the danger these jobs put my companions into. I hung the wreath around the sketch and said, "I'll always remember you, friend," under my breath.

Every time I go into what the people of Anglachel call "The Jungle of Despair," I can never figure out what people think is so disparaging about it. It is a lush jungle with the tallest trees and the wildest vines adorned with some of the most vibrant flowers I'd ever seen. It brings me back to my childhood when my grandmother would take me on diplomatic visits to the Spring Maiden's Duchy. My grandmother was always jealous of how much people would compliment the Spring Maiden's garden because it was so bright and colorful. As a young girl, I was often left alone outside to play. I would lose myself in the pastels while my grandmother argued over some treaty or whatever.

However, for all the beauty and magic I remembered from the Spring Maiden's garden, it couldn't hold a candle to this jungle. The Spring Maiden's garden was lovely, but it was also orderly and organized. The jungle was wild. The vines would wrap around the trees or lay along the jungle floor in no particular pattern. Some vines would be full of blooms, and some would be completely barren. Some trees would grow straight up into the sky, while some trees would twist and bend in wild directions. This jungle reminded me why I came here. I didn't want to be tamed, I wanted to be free.

Before I lost myself in the trees, I directed my attention back to Pegutsai. She had been expertly darting around the brambles, and the rest of us just had to follow. I'd always heard stories about adventurers traveling through thick jungles like this by cutting a path, Pegutsai knew the jungle well enough that we didn't have to damage the wildlife. I loved it. It felt like we were sneaking through secret passages. I stayed in the back of the group so that I could make sure to keep an eye on Traci. She struggled a bit more than the rest of us. She didn't need to be flexible when she teleports everywhere. But she was keeping up. I was proud of her.

Traci's hand grasped a branch to her right, and I saw two small glints creeping down toward her hand. I slid down the muddy incline and swatted up with the broadside of my sword. The snake went flying through the air, and the branch snapped. I scooped Traci up and continued sliding down the incline, stopping at an adjacent tree.

"What the hell, Ash?" Traci rounded on me.

"There was a snake about to bite you! I was saving you!" I said, defending myself.

"You think I didn't see it? It was halfway up the branch. I wasn't planning on staying there long enough for it to get to me."

"I just didn't want to take any chances."

Traci gave me the same look of pity and acceptance I'd gotten many times this past year. "I know, Ash, but you've got to let me make my own decisions."

I knew what she meant. I had been jumpy lately and swooping in without thinking. She needed to be able to act for herself when were on jobs. I took a step back and a deep breath.

"You're right. I'm sorry," I relented.

The rest of the journey was pretty uneventful until we came to a wide river. As Traci and I approached, Pegutsai had begun testing the strength of the long vines.

"We're going to have to swing across," she explained. "Are you going to be o.k.?" She asked, looking at Traci.

"Yeah, it's fine," Traci said. "I can just teleport across. No big deal."

I didn't like the sound of that. "Shouldn't you save your teleports in case we actually have to fight?"

"I mean, one shouldn't take too much of my magic," Traci assured me.

"Let's be safe. You know that I could swing both of us across. We just have to tie you to me," I suggested.

"You're sure that will work?" Traci questioned. "You'll be fine?"

"C'mon,, babe, you know me. I've got this," I boasted.

We used some rope to tie us together. Duri used some knots I'd never seen before to make sure Traci was secure. I let Pegutsai and Duri go first. They had to switch vines about three times to make it across. I watched the rapids of the river rage below. I couldn't let us fall. Traci was in so tight, she'd have no way to swim free from it. I bounced on the balls of my feet a couple of times to try and get used to the new weight. Traci wasn't heavy, but she was a bit bigger than me. That means she more than doubled the weight I was used to when I'd do this sort of thing. I was starting to get a little nervous, but I still knew it was smarter for Traci to conserve her magic.

"You o.k.?" Traci asked. She could probably feel my heart racing since she was snug against my back.

"Yeah, just getting excited," I lied.

Pegutsai and Duri had safely made it across, and it was our turn. I took several steps back so I could get a running jump. I raced towards the river bank and used the momentum to propel us forward as I grabbed the first vine. We shot forward like an arrow freshly loosed from a bow. Our arch was much faster than I'd anticipated. We reached the peak of the swing in a matter of seconds. I quickly readjusted and took hold of the next vine. It wasn't ready for the sudden shift and took a wide swerve to the right. I suddenly didn't know where we were going, because the vine was heading to an open space, away from the other hanging vines. I released a panicked inhale that Traci must have heard.

"Don't worry, I've got this," she said. Suddenly, the added weight disappeared from my back. Traci must have teleported to the other side of the bank. I used the opportunity to take a wild leap toward a bundle of vines straight ahead. I'd made it, and I was able to scurry my way across to my waiting companions.

I rushed up to Traci and took her into my arms.

"I'm so sorry. I don't know what I was thinking," I cried.

"It's o.k., Ash. I'm sorry too. I know you wanted me to save my magic," she apologized.

"No, it's my fault. I'm so scared all the time. I don't want to lose you," I finally said out loud.

"Ash, I'm not going anywhere," she said, confused.

"No, not like that. I just want to make sure you're safe."

"I know what you mean. I miss The Scourge too." That eased the constant pit that had been in my stomach. "But this is our life. We chose to be adventurers. I know what I signed up for, and you have to let me live my life."

"I'm just so scared," I repeated.

"Me too. I don't want to die or lose you, or Duri, or Pegutsai. But if this is going to work, we have to trust each other. And trust each other to make our own decisions," she pleaded.

"I just miss him so much," I said. I began to cry and rested my head on her shoulder.

"I know, Ash, I know," she said.

Chapter Seven

Would That Really Be So Bad?

Traci

"It's for a set of twins, magic users in The Slums," Ulani said, finishing the job offer. Ulani was a Mascara with yellow skin and antlers like a deer. She'd been giving us job tips for the past couple of years.

"It's a lot of gold, Trace," Asha commented.

"But we don't really need the gold, Ash," I reminded her. As I started getting older, and Asha really didn't, we started to settle down a little bit. We'd made a good bit of coin adventuring, and bought a house on the northeast side of Middle Anglachel. Many of our companions were able to retire, and about as many weren't so lucky. Now that it was just the two of us again, we were able to be pretty selective on the jobs we took. "Is this really the kind of job we want? What did they even do?"

"The official job offer doesn't say, it just has their names and descriptions," Ulani answered.

"I think you know I'm not asking about the official job offer. You've had to have heard people talk about them," I said, trying to coax the truth out of her.

"Only because it's you, Miss Traci," Ulani sighed. "You know you've always reminded me of my mother."

I could have done without that last bit. I really didn't think about the long-term consequences of being in love with an Elf. It was getting pretty annoying when people started mistaking me for Asha's aunt or mother. We were the same age, but she only looked about three years older than when I'd first met her. To most people, at least. I could always see the years of pain and hardship in her.

"People say that they're messing with the balance of power in the city," Ulani began. "See, the girl, Quinn, she can do necromancy magic. She's been using it to heal people in The Slums. It's taking business away from the doctors in the market. The boy, Quincy, he can do Holy magic. He's been putting blessings on people, and they've been staying healthier. The factory owners in the Business District hate it."

"Why?" Asha asked. "I thought all they cared about were productivity. Wouldn't they be happy that their workers can come in more often?"

"If you're going to pick 'em this young, Miss Traci, you should at least make sure they're smart," Ulani said with a laugh. Asha looked back at me and smiled. She thought it was funny when someone called her young.

"Why don't you go ahead and answer her question, Ulani?" I said.

"Sure, sure. The factories count on their staff getting sick or breaking down by the time they reach middle age. If they quit before they get old, they can trade them in for someone younger. If their staff stays healthy, they're going to get old. Even if they stay as productive, they have to pay them more for their years of experience," Ulani explained.

"So the millionaires in the city want to nip this in the bud before they lose too much money," I reasoned.

"That's evil," Asha said.

"Maybe she is smart," Ulani said.

"You said they are magic users, but they live in The Slums. Did they go to Arcana University on a scholarship?" I asked.

"No, no, Miss Traci. These two aren't even old enough to have started the university. They must have been born with their magic."

That struck a chord. "So they're like me."

"What do you think, Trace?" Asha asked.

"Let's take the job," I told Ulani.

"Really? You gonna take them down?" Ulani said, surprised.

"Something like that," I said.

Ulani gave us all the information she had about the job. After the 30 years we'd been adventuring, my magic had gotten leagues stronger, and Asha finally stopped worrying so much about me using up my power. I teleported us to a fancy office in the Business District, and we negotiated a higher rate with the client. Apparently, they really do pay more for experience. I made sure the contract worded that we would "take care" of them. I've learned that vague wording is a lifesaver in these kinds of jobs. I teleported us to the edge of The Slums, and we began walking to the location of the twins' most recent pop-up clinic.

"We're saving them, right?" Asha said, knowing the answer already.

"Of course," I said. "These two are obviously doing what they think is the right thing. They shouldn't be killed for that. You know the other adventurers in town wouldn't think twice about it."

"Oh, I know," Asha said. "And they'll be great assets. Necromancy and Holy magic are pretty rare. Especially when it's innate; think of how easy it would be to clear out undead with them!"

"This isn't a recruitment trip. We want to help them choose what they want for themselves," I chided Asha. She'd been like this for a few years now. I knew she loved me, but it felt like everybody else was a resource for her. She'd stopped caring about anyone that wasn't us.

"Sure, but you know they'll want to be adventurers," Asha countered. "What kind of a life is there for two young people with powerful magic that's not this life?"

"I don't know," I said. "Maybe we could pay for them to get into the university?"

"Are we adopting these kids?!" Asha guffawed.

"Would that really be so bad?" I asked. "To have a couple of people to look after us when we grow old?"

"I think you mean when *you* grow old," Asha said.

"You're just as old as I am," I reminded her. "You're going to start slowing down, too."

"Whatever you say, babe," Asha said before jogging ahead to check the cross street in front of us.

This was far from our first time in the slums, but it was always a little unsettling. Since my family lived in North Angalchel, I had always heard about the rampant crime in The Slums. As I'd gotten older, I realized that it was mostly because the majority of non-Humans and darker-skinned Humans lived in The Slums. It is wild to realize how deeply engrained a lot of this stuff is. I'm sure the fact that The Slums is also the home of rampant poverty is also a factor. The streets aren't as well-kept, the houses aren't as well-maintained, and the people are, I'll say, less refined. I had learned to find the beauty in The Slums over the years. Most of it lay with its people.

It took us a while to ask around and figure out where the twins would be, but we eventually got word they would be setting up a pop-up clinic that night in an abandoned warehouse at The Docks.

"Why's it always a warehouse in The Docks?" Asha asked.

"You've gotta love the classics," I said. "At least they're not doing evil things there."

We had taken out more than our fair share of criminal activity in The Docks. The Docks are adjacent to The Slums, but it is mostly the center of shipping operations in Anglachel. That also leads to an increased level of business activity compared to The Slums. The shadiest folks in Anglachel have learned that if you want to stay out of sight, passing through The Slums is the most effective way to accomplish that. I resented how right they were.

"What they're doing is still illegal, Trace," Asha reminded me. "They don't have a permit to run a magic business here. What the rich guys are doing is wrong, but that doesn't make what they're doing right."

"Since when did you care so much about the law? Aren't you the same Asha Alistar that stole 5,000 gold from the bank of Anglachel because a teller was rude to you once?" I asked.

"It was for more than that, but yeah, pretty much," She admitted. "O.K., so they're helping people illegally, who cares? They probably don't know any better."

I grinned and nodded in approval. "Now you're getting it."

"Let's go adopt these kids!" Asha said, racing ahead and throwing her fist into the air.

Hearing her say it made me feel warm inside. She actually wanted to let new people into our life. Really let them in. Maybe she wasn't changing so much after all.

We finally found the warehouse. It was, as expected, the most blighted one we could find. I'm pretty sure we've been to this exact warehouse at least three times in the past decade. We decided I should go in first. I could teleport in and try to explain what we were doing here. Asha would sneak in the back and provide backup if they weren't initially receptive to our offer.

I looked through the front window, and I spotted a locked door outlined in light. They were here. I teleported to the door and knocked.

A high-pitched feminine voice called out from behind the door. "Look, I don't know how you got in here, but we're not open yet."

"Quinn, I'm here to speak with you. I think you'll want to hear what I have to say," I called through the door.

"Lady, I don't know who you are, but we are busy," a similarly high-pitched masculine voice yelled.

"I'm giving you a chance to come out here on your own. I don't want to drag you out of here," I tried. I didn't want to threaten them, but they were clearly already on guard.

"Try us, lady," Quincy snapped.

I teleported the door off its hinges to reveal the twins setting up chairs in a large room. They were just setting up for the clinic. They were Humans with light skin and dark hair. Quincy's hair was combed to the left side and draped in front of his eyes. Quinn's hair was long, with bangs perfectly framing her face. They were really thin. Free clinics must pay as much as it sounds.

"I warned you!" Quincy shouted at me. He lifted his hand towards me, and it began to glow with a bright light.

"I wouldn't if I were you," Asha's voice growled. She was suddenly standing behind Quincy with a sword held to his throat.

"Please, we don't want any trouble," Quinn said, panicked. "We just want to help people."

"I know that," I said, trying to reassure her. "We don't want any trouble either."

"Your friend's sword tells a different story," Quincy said. His eyes were moving wildly, trying to catch a glimpse of his assailant without actually moving his head.

"Drop your hand, and I'll move the blade away from under your chin," Asha said authoritatively.

Quinn and Quincy looked each other in the eyes for what felt like an eternity. Finally, Quincy lowered his hand.

"Was that so hard?" Asha asked, slowly returning the blade to its scabbard.

"They're scared, give them a little slack," I begged her.

Asha held her hands up, relenting to me. "Fine."

"Who are you? What are you doing here?" Quinn asked carefully, not sure what she was supposed to do.

"We were hired by some really powerful people in this city. They don't like what you're doing in The Slums," I explained, trying to keep any inflection out of my voice. I wanted to give them the information without giving away what we thought about it.

"So why not just kill us?" Quincy asked. "Clearly, the two of you could have just done that without much trouble."

Asha audibly laughed from the back of the room. "You got that right."

"I'm like you," I explained. "I was born with the power to use spatial magic. I know what it's like not to understand your own power."

"We don't need your help," Quincy said a little too quickly,

"Quinc, I would like to learn how to control my power," she said, pleading with her brother. "I almost made Mrs. Meadows a zombie. What would we have done if that happened?"

"We'd have figured it out. I could have blasted it with my Holy magic," Quincy said.

"And kill everyone at the clinic? You've never been able to control your blasts either," Quinn retorted.

I began slowly walking up to Quinn.

"I can help you," I said. "It has taken me years to learn how to control my magic. I can teach you how I did it."

"Why would you help us? Do these 'powerful people' want to use us?" Quincy asked.

"I'm sure they'd love to," Asha quipped. "But we don't. We want to make them think you've been taken out. We'll still get paid, but we can help the two of you build a new life."

"Why should we trust you?" Quincy asked, narrowing his eyes at Asha.

"Maybe because I didn't kill you when I had the chance?" Asha offered. "If you don't trust us, you're going to die. Not at our hands, but they're just going to hire someone else. After decades of doing this, I can confidently say we're the most merciful mercenaries in the business."

"Decade? How old are you? You look like you're our age?" Quinn questioned.

"We'll explain everything," I said. "But we have to get out of here. If we could find you, it is only a matter of time until someone else does too."

"Could we do the clinic?" Quincy asked, suddenly more sincere. "There are people counting on us. This can be our last one, but there are promises we made last time that I want to keep."

"Asha, what do you say? Can we play bodyguard for one night?" I asked.

"Honestly," Asha began, "Sounds like fun."

"O.K., so we have a deal?" I asked. "We keep you and your patients safe for one night, and you'll come with us."

"Deal," Quinn said, clearly before her brother could chime in.

I felt really good. We'd done it. We saved two kids, and Asha seemed willing to get to know them better. I started to feel like my worry might have been misguided. I might have been seeing things in Asha that I expected to see instead of what was actually there. She pulled Quincy aside, and it made me smile. She must have seen some of herself in him. I certainly did.

"So you're interested in learning more about zombies?" I overheard her ask him.

Chapter Eight

For the Rest of Your Life

IT'S NOT ALWAYS EASY being an Elf in a Human world. They never use enough seasoning on their food. It feels like all of their cultural traditions revolve around money. They keep saying things like "life is short" when it just isn't for me. They just grow old too fast. When someone says they'll love you for the rest of their life, you like to think that they'll be around for the rest of yours. For an Elf in a Human world, that just isn't how things work.

Traci and I have lived what many in Galevyn would consider a full life. We've made many friends and lost about half as many in the end. We made a lot of money and bought a house. We raised two teenage magic users into successful adult adventurers. We even saved the world a couple of times. We were two very accomplished individuals, but Traci was nearing the end of her life, and I still have several centuries left in me. I loved this place because it moved so fast; now I understood why.

Traci's lying in our bed right now, and the doctors say she could go at any minute. It's so bizarre. She doesn't even seem that sick. She's just old. It is so confusing that this woman, one of the most powerful women on the planet, can leave it the same way as everyone else. Didn't we do enough to earn her more time? Was there something else we could have done?

The door to our bedroom opens, and Quincy walks out. He's become a lot closer to us ever since his sister died. His face looks like he's come to terms with what is happening. He is still sad, but there is some sense of acceptance there.

"You should go see her," he tells me.

"I know," I respond.

"She's getting worse. You should be by her side," he says, telling me things I already know.

I slowly stand up and make my way to the door. He puts his hand on my shoulder and pulls me in for a hug.

"I know this is hard, mom. We'll get through this together," he reassures me.

I return the hug and consider what he said. He expects me to stick around. He wants me to watch him grow old and leave me too. I rest my head on his shoulder and consider this. How much do I owe him? I lift my head and nod, trying to conceal my indecisiveness. I walk into the room, and I see her.

It is so strange how, thinking back, she looks nothing like the girl I met on the campus of Arcana University. Even so, every time I look at her, all I see is my Traci. The woman that stood by me even when I made the wrong choices. The woman who made me better by calling me out when I needed it. The woman I love more than any other person I've ever met. My Traci.

"Hi, Ash," she groans when she sees me approach.

"You look great, babe," I say. I mean it. As I said, I see her for who she is, and she'll always be beautiful to me.

"Yeah, but I don't hold a candle to you. What did I do to deserve to grow old with someone as incredible as you?" She asks.

This is too much. I can feel tears forming at the bottom of my eyes.

"I could ask you the same thing," I say, sitting in the chair next to her bed and grasping her hand.

"Can you sit with me?" she asks.

"For the rest of your life," I agree, knowing it won't be much longer.

"I love you, Ash," she says with one of her final breaths.

"I love you too, Trace," I reply. I lean in and kiss her. Really kiss her. Her head lifts to meet mine, even though she doesn't really have the strength. I want to hold onto this moment for as long as I can.

I don't know how long we held hands. It could have been minutes. It could have been hours, hell, it could have been days. All I know is that I eventually fell asleep, and when I woke up, she was gone. Her body was still there, obviously, but Traci was gone.

I walked to our closet and grabbed a pre-packed bag I keep in there. It has several days worth of clothing, adventuring supplies, and enough gold to last me for a few months. I walk to the corner of our room and fasten my sword harness to my belt. I flashback to the moment I strapped the sword around my ridiculous ball gown before leaving the fey realm. I guess this is the start of a new chapter for me.

I walk out of our room, and I see Quincy sitting there. I dig the house keys out of my pocket.

"The house is yours, Quinc," I tell him, handing him the keys.

"You can't leave, mom. You have to process this. We need to make arrangements for her funeral together," He says.

"You know that I don't work like that. I appreciate you so much. You and your sister reminded me that connections are worth making, but I can't stay here. I can't see her in every wood grain on the floor, every room, every person," I say, touching his cheek. "I can't lose you, Quincy. I want to live believing you're still out there, somewhere. I want to be able to pretend that in 50 years, there's still someone I love living a fulfilling life."

"I can't understand. I don't think I could ever understand, but I believe you," he says. "Find happiness, mom. Don't give up on people. Make friends, fall in love again."

"I will," I say, knowing that I'll never let myself fall in love again.

I hug him one last time and walk out the door. I risk one final look back. I see myself carrying Traci across the threshold. I see Quinn and Quincy seeing the house for the first time and confiding in us that this will be the first time either of them will have their own bedroom. I see all 25 adventuring companions that walked through our door at some point in the last 40-some years. Then I turn around and face the road before me. I won't forget these memories, but I can't dwell on them. There's a lot of life ahead of me.

Chapter Nine

Keep Moving Forward

"YOU ARE SO BEAUTIFUL," Rio whispered into my ear as he moved his smooth hand from the back of my head to the small of my back. I took a deep breath and drank him in. He smelled like sweat and myrrh from the oils he used in his rituals. The scents clung to his thick chest hair. I saw his muscles tense under his tan skin, and he released a held breath just before he rolled over onto the bedroll spread out in our tent.

"You're incredible," he told me for the fifth time that day.

I sat up and began putting my clothes back on, then I looked back at him and flashed a grin. "You may have mentioned that before."

He looked up at me with sad puppy dog eyes. "C'mon, Asha. You don't have to leave. You could lay here with me for a little while. We only just set up camp. We have time."

He's not the first partner to say something like this to me. I hoped I could talk him out of it. I'd hate to have to shut this down before we'd completed the job. That'd be awkward as hell.

"We agreed this was just about fun, didn't we?"

"Of course, but I just hoped. . uh . . . I mean . . " he began to stumble. He's especially cute when he's frazzled. His rolling Reyes accent is still attractive when it doesn't know what to say. This wasn't helping.

"We can talk later," I said evanescently, hoping he'll forget this conversation happened.

I finished the last buckle on my black leather armor and walked out of the tent. My long dark hair was down and still a bit of a mess. Lisel and Ricci were sitting around the fire. Lisel is a Halfling alchemist, meaning she makes things that heal us and things that hurt our enemies. I've worked with a lot of different magic users in my century and a half of adventuring, and she's the first that doesn't actually perform it. She stores it in bottles. I still don't really understand magic. She's a traditional mother friend, always trying to look out for us. Her look complements her personality, with smudges covering her clothes and her chestnut hair sticking out in all directions. Ricci is a red Mascara with rounded goat-like horns outlining his surprisingly soft facial features. He has raven black hair and a rough beard. He does most of the upfront fighting for our group.

I sidle up to the fire and take a seat on a rock. "So what are we thinking? Will we make it to Ahranai tomorrow morning?"

We're in Kapoor tracking down a High Priest of a Quietus cult. He has been terrorizing a small town called Ahranai, and the town secretly commissioned a job posting through the thieves guild to stop him. Lisel, Ricci, and Rio were surprised that I wanted to do something that seemed so altruistic for such low pay, but the truth is that I take every opportunity I can to leave Anglachel. Too many memories there.

"I'm thinking you should start taking it easier on our paladin," Ricci's deep growl of a voice teased. "Some of his screams started to worry me."

I laughed with him. "You probably won't need to worry about that much longer."

"Take it easy on her," Lisel said, slapping Ricci with the back of her hand. "Yes, Asha, we should make it to Ahranai by tomorrow morning. Have either of you thought about strategy?"

Ricci straightened his posture, suddenly serious. "I spent a lot of time in Ahranai in my youth. I know the city layout pretty well. That should be to our advantage."

"Yes, good. Asha, what have you prepared?"

"Wait, no, we're not just going to move on. Ricci, you grew up in Ahranai? How are we just now hearing about this?" I asked.

I looked into his eyes, and his seriousness was still holding, but only just. "I didn't grow up in Ahranai. But I used to visit family there. It's not a big deal. We don't need to talk about it."

"Of course," Lisel said, trying to keep the meeting on track. "Now, Asha. What do you think will be the best strategy to draw out the high priest?"

"Oh, we're going to talk about it," I said, continuing the conversation I wanted to have. When you don't actually get that close to anybody, it is pretty fun to dig into their pasts. "I didn't even know there were still Mascara in Kapoor. I thought they got rooted out during the River Elves' partition."

"Well, my bubbe was always stubborn. Her family had lived in that house for generations, and she wasn't going to get shoved out for being different."

"I get that, but how could she have stopped them? I've heard stories from other Mascara about some pretty brutal treatment when they resisted the River Elves."

Surprisingly, that question brought a smile to his face. "She was born with the ability to use barrier magic, and she'd mastered it enough to hold a barrier around the house." Obviously, this was a point of family pride for him.

I whistled, acknowledging how impossible what he was describing must have been. "She sounds like a spitfire." She reminded me of Traci. I blinked hard to shut the memory out of my head.

"She is," Ricci said, settling back into his serious posture to continue the strategy meeting.

"But yeah, I'm prepared to fight. I plan to sneak around and slit the high priest's throat when he comes out. You know what I do," I finally contributed.

"Thank you for all your preparation," Lisel said sarcastically. "Did anyone put any thought into how we'd draw him out?"

Rio slinked out of the tent and sat next to me, a little closer than I would have preferred. "I could pretend to be a paladin of Quietus. That should certainly pique his interest."

"Thank you, Rio," Lisel commended. "That is an actual idea."

***

The following morning we packed up and made our way down the dirt road to Ahranai. Lisel was right. It wasn't long until we saw buildings in the distance. Unexpectedly, we also saw smoke rising from the inland side of the town. Before any of us could ask any questions, Ricci took off in that direction. I chased after him because I knew I was the only one that could keep up with the most athletic member of our party. I looked back to see Lisel give me a nod, acknowledging she understood that I'd look out for him if anything came up. We ran until we pushed into a smoke cloud. I slowed down to assess what we were running into, but Ricci didn't stop. He reached the charred remains of a house that had crumbled on itself. He threw himself into the ashes and began digging through the rubble. I carefully approached him and knelt down.

"Ricci, what's going on?" I said in the most neutral tone I could manage.

"Bubbe. . . . This is where . . . What if she . . . " he stammered. Gods. This neighborhood was where his grandmother lived. This was a massive attack, and there is pretty much no way she made it out.

I put my hand on his shoulder. "Ricci, buddy, we need to get out of this smoke before we lose our breath. You've got to be feeling it."

He continued to mindlessly dig, but I could see him breathing much heavier. I put my hands on either side of his face and forced him to look at me.

"We'll figure out what happened, but we can't do that if we're dead. Let's get out of here and ask around."

He slowly nodded, and I helped him stand up. I still couldn't see any trace of his firm foundation that our group had learned to rely on. He was fragile. Broken. I was familiar with that feeling. I wrapped my arm around his torso and walked him out of the blackened hull of his bubbe's neighborhood.

When we emerged into the fresh air, Rio and Lisel were there to meet us.

Rio rushed up. Gods, I could not deal with his doting now. "Is he o.k.? Ricci, are you o.k.? You look burnt."

Oh, he was checking on Ricci. That was refreshing.

"He's fine, he just panicked." I didn't know how much Ricci wanted me to say yet.

"Yes. I'm fine," Ricci said. His countenance shifted from worry to determination. "We need to find who did this."

"I'll ask around," I offered. Lisel and Rio were better at the emotional stuff anyway. Getting answers was something I could do. I slipped away before anyone could object. I risked a look back and I saw them entering an inn at the edge of town.

I began asking around town, and it didn't take too many questions to learn that the spirited older Mascara woman living in that neighborhood didn't make it out. She seemed to become a fixture of the town. She was the only one willing to stand up to the high priest; clearly, this destruction was how he felt about it. They said the entire neighborhood went up in flames at the same time. She lived in the middle, with everything around her on fire, she never stood a chance. This was very targeted. The city had already dug through her house, and they couldn't find any substantial remains, just ash. Regular fire can't do that, this had to be magic. I was tempted to go after the high priest on my own, but Ricci needed to see this through. He deserved that much.

I returned to the inn to see the three of them sitting around the common room. Kapoor has always been known for its colorful and elaborate patterns. This room was no different. It featured two couches with an orange repeating circular pattern. As I got closer, I could see it was an artistic representation of leaves. Life is full of ironies. The couches were facing a crackling fireplace. It looked like the inn had closed off this room to give us some space. Based on their faces, Ricci had filled the other two in on what he presumed happened.

Lisel looked up at me as I approached. "What did you find out?"

"This was them, the Quietus cult. It was definitely a magical fire, and apparently, Ricci's bubbe was pushing back against their demands."

"That sounds like her. Did she … ?" The question faded before he could say the words. I just shook my head. He didn't need to hear me say it. It would just make it hurt more. His eyes were still focused, but I saw moisture gather at the base of them. I walked up and sat beside him. I just wanted to be here for him, whatever he needed.

"We can take the night off," Lisel concluded. "If they just acted, that should buy us some time before their next move. Let's get some rest."

"No!" Ricci shouted. "We have to do something now."

"Yes," Lisel agreed. "We do have to do something now. I have to prepare some alchemist fire and potions for the upcoming assault. Rio needs to finish the Quietus alterations to his armor. Asha needs to continue asking around to learn what she can about the cultists. You need to take a beat. You are of no use to us if you can't think clearly. Let yourself grieve, at least a little bit, then you can help us when the time comes."

Rio stood up, taking Lisel's cue to walk out of the room to work on his disguise. Lisel looked at me like she was trying to figure out what I was feeling. I didn't want to think too much about the emotions this was brewing inside of me, but her eyes were pulling it out of me.

"It's never easy," I finally said. Ricci turned towards me, tears visibly rolling down his face. "To lose someone. I've lost my fair share of people in my life. Some of them meant a lot to me, probably as much as your bubbe meant to you. And one of them certainly meant more."

Now I could feel tears welling up on my face. For the first time in decades, I didn't push it down.

"It doesn't matter how they go; it never seems fair. It always feels like a personal attack, like the gods are playing some sort of cruel joke on you. I mean, they put people into my life for what? To take them away? How does that make sense? But we have to keep moving forward. That's all we can do."

Massive tears were now pouring down my face and I could hear the breaks they caused in my voice. I couldn't believe I was being this vulnerable.

"She's right, Ricci. We have to keep moving forward, for those we've lost. We have to live the best life we can, because they can't. Because that is what they'd want," Lisel said, clearly speaking to both of us. For some reason, her words made me feel angry.

"How do you know what she'd want!" I screamed irrationally loud. "I held her hand as she died. I watched the life leave her body. The last thing she told me was that she loved me. She didn't say anything about what kind of life I was supposed to lead."

"Did you know my grandma?" Ricci said, clearly still disoriented. Lisel looked confused too, but she was trying to follow what I was saying.

"How long ago was this?" She asked me gently.

"64 years, three months, and twelve days," I said, almost automatically, brushing my hair behind my elven ears with my hand.

Lisel stood up and threw her arms around me. "Oh, Ash. You've held this in for that long?"

I couldn't say anything. Her Halfling height meant I could still see over her head. I looked in Ricci's direction, and his eyes had gone wide, clearly trying to understand all the revelations I'd just thrown at him. The expression on his face was ridiculous, especially with the tear tracks still visible on his cheeks. He looked like a crying child suddenly surprised by a new dog. It made me laugh.

"What is it?" his low voice rumbled.

"Your face," I managed through my hysterical bouts of hysteria.

His hand began to feel around his face. Lisel looked at him and started to laugh too.

"What?" he asked.

"She's right, your expression. It's not like you," Lisel explained.

Ricci didn't seem to understand, but at this point, the laughter was contagious. He joined us, and we sat there laughing with each other. I felt like I was releasing 64 years of built-up tension. After a few minutes, we regained our composure.

Lisel slapped my arm with the back of her hand. "You've got to tell people your secrets. If this is going to work, we have to trust each other."

I smiled at hearing Traci's words repeated to me. I resisted the urge to push her out of my mind, and I allowed her memory to comfort me.

"I trust you," I said to Lisel and Ricci, and I meant it. I'd been moving through life like a ghost. Jumping from group to group and never forming any real attachments. I remembered the day I'd lost Traci and Quincy urging me to make friends and fall in love again. I owed it to Traci to try. I still didn't know if I could fall in love, but I could start letting people in again.

"You guys want to hear how an Elven Princess of Autumn traveled to Galevyn to become an adventurer?"

"That sounds like a story my bubbe would have loved," Ricci said.

I didn't want to lose these people, but I finally remembered what it felt like to have someone to lose.

"My Aunt Poppy was an adventurer, and she'd always tell me stories about this realm. One day, I was
dueling with her . . . . "

About the Author

Terry Bartley is the founder and creative director of Starlight King Press and a journalism, literature, and English teacher at Scott High School. He is the host of Most Writers are Fans, a podcast about the intersection of writing and fandom, and Ink Over AI, which explores how writers can engage ethically and responsibly with AI without outsourcing their creativity. His work has appeared in the Coal Valley News and Screenrant.

He loves tabletop roleplaying games, reading comics, and watching TV shows starring complicated women. He lives in rural West Virginia with his dog, Etsy.

His debut novel, Destined for Greater Things will debut in Summer 2026.

Acknowledgments

THIS BOOK CAME TOGETHER because I got tired of editing my first novel and wanted to start writing again. I didn't want to write a sequel to the novel, because I hadn't plotted out the potential series yet. I decided I would write short stories about side characters, or characters tangentially connected to the main characters in the novel. I ended up using these stories as a way to flesh out and fully build the fantasy world of Galevyn. Along the way, I fell in love with Asha, Karuk, and Rowena (and Gin, he's a blast to write).

That's how this book came together. But I never could have done it without the help and encouragement of a lot of incredible people.

The first person I have to think is my best friend, Dustin Whitman. He has been my biggest cheerleader and had been keeping me accountable every step of the way. We've been jokingly referring to him as my agent, but I think that somewhere along the way it might have actually happened.

I also need to give a giant thank you to my brother, Allen Bartley. I have literally bounced literally every idea, character, plot point, and storyline off of him. He probably isn't reading this because I'm sure he's tired of hearing about these characters by now and he could probably recite every story in here.

I'd like to thank my writing buddies and grammar friends, Robb Livinggood, Heather Pettry, Brandie Newsom, Angela Jones, and Heather Hayes. You all helped make me look good and also talk through every weird fantasy grammar question I had.

My editor Erin Bledsoe, thank you for helping me get some perspective on my characters and making sure readers know every setting isn't a white void. Bethany Atazadeh, I don't know you, but your Youtube videos gave me the confidence to put all this together. Thank you to Ariel Price and Mike Pereira for your design advice. My writing colleagues and mentors, Sam J. Miller, Cody Walker, Kirsha Fox, Andrea Fink, and Amada Ross, thank you for all your advice and for making me feel like I'm part of a larger community. To the band, Sub-Radio, thank you for your constant inspiration.

Finally, thank you to Sandra Bartley, Betty Oquendo, Audrey Sands, Sara Price, Jeff McNeely, Mackenzie

Price, Dan Taylor, Chase Henderson, Rachel Henderson, Eric Hager, AJ Smith, and Melinda Piccirillo for helping me feel like I could do this and for all of the intangible ways you helped me throughout this process. I'm sure there are people I left out and for that I'm sorry and please know that I appreciate you too!

Thanks for reading!

*You **didn't think an** arranged marriage was going to stop her, did you? If Asha's story meant something to you, the best thing you can do is leave a review on Amazon or Goodreads. For an indie author, that's worth more than a sacred artifact.*

Asha's story isn't over. Find out what became of the princess who ran away from everything in Destined for Greater Things, coming August 2026 — including the son who inherited her spirit.

Twitter: @terrybartley

TikTok: @terrlet

Instagram: @terrlet

Facebook: @terrybartleywriter

Podcast: Most Writers Are Fans

Destined for Greater Things

Coming Summer 2026

Celeste

I woke up with the sun shining through my eastward-facing window. Since I was a child, my bed has been on the west side of the room so that I always wake up with the rising sun. I've always felt it was important to be awake at the break of dawn, ensuring I maximize daylight hours for maximum productivity.

I slept on the same side of the bed that I do every night to ensure I followed the same ritual each morning. I looked over the chalkboard hanging on that side of the room, it always features my daily to-do list. Today's agenda primarily focuses on my long-term goal of determining the source of Creation magic. Obviously, I know that the churches of the gods Hwedo and Lovelace claim that power stems from their divine patrons, but I reject the idea that a handful of "all-powerful" gods supply all the magic on Planet Galevyn. I'd already pinpointed that Illusion magic seems to pull energy from an area in the ocean between the Anglachel and Ferreira continents. Once I pinpoint the power centers of all schools of magic, I'll present my findings to Arcana University. With any luck, they'll fund an expedition to uncover these power sources. I want to be known for more than being famed inventor and entrepreneur Anthony Magister's daughter.

I made my bed and finished by placing the decorative pillows on the foot of my bed. I hated adding unnecessary decorative flourishes to my living quarters, but my father insisted. I had learned to pick my battles with him, and if putting frilly pillows on top of my practical comforter would make my father more likely to consider my most imperative requests, I'd add a little lace to my morning routine.

I turned away from my bed and walked straight ahead to my wardrobe. It is full of elegant gowns my father deems necessary for most occasions, but on days like today, when my father is out of town on business, I relished the opportunity to wear my work gear. A grin crossed my face as I reached for my plain black t-shirt and work overalls. I completed the ensemble with a pair of sturdy work boots.

It was now time to work on my hair. My natural hair is very thick and curly, and managing it is the only part of my day that forces me to do any real work on my appearance. If I left it alone, it would stick out everywhere, get in my eyes, and potentially get caught in whatever experiments I had lined up. I looked into the mirror beside my bed and couldn't believe how poofy it had gotten overnight. I took a deep breath and pulled out my bottle of hair oil. I began the tedious process of combing oil through my hair to make it manageable. After what felt like an eternity, I was finally ready to put my hair up. After much experimentation, I'd learned the easiest way to manage it is a high loose bun towards the top of my head. While my hair was up, I used more oil to tamp down the remaining hairs on the edge of my hairline. Finally, I really wanted to see some of my hair's natural waves, so I loosened the bun ever so slightly to fluff it out just a bit. Moments like these, I feel really envious of the lighter-skinned human women who have more manageable natural hair.

Finally, the woman looking back at me in the mirror was an accurate reflection of how I see myself. My dark brown provides a subtle contrast to the black clothing, my hair looks natural but controlled, and my clothes are loose and practical. I gauged the position of the sun in the window and was pleased I managed to do all of this in about an hour.

I walked downstairs to my magic lab. Some people say walking through an empty mansion is creepy, but I always find it refreshing. Whenever my father is here, he seems to be conducting business at all hours. It is impossible to find a quiet moment. I love walking through the vast hallways of our family home while only hearing the sound of my boots against the marble floors. I have the feeling today is going to be a good day.

I made it into my lab and laid out all the things I'd need for my research. First, I take out all of the non-magical items. These are things like an oversized globe of Galevyn, a series of bottles to capture magic essence, and all of the scrolls and books I'd been using to dig into the specifics of creation magic. Lastly, I strapped on a backpack that houses my very mechanical camera so I could capture any important discoveries. I could use a crystal imbued with identification magic to take pictures, but the camera is more reliable for me.

Next, for the magical items, I have to be much more careful.

I have a rare condition that I have to keep vigilant about if I don't want to spend endless gold on magic items. My body naturally produces an anti-magic field that negates any magic that gets near me. When I end up face-to-face with an evil spell-throwing wizard, this is a really handy ability. However, living in a world that is almost entirely run by magical items, my day-to-day can get a bit complicated. I have to make sure I don't shop in stores that use basic charms on their doors that make them automatically open. If I get too close, which often means just walking through the door, the charm is dispelled, and the owner will have to pay to get a new one installed. I can't risk petting my friend's rescue animals. There is no way to know if they may have been conjured by a wizard and since abandoned. If I touch a conjured animal, it just disappears, sent back to where it originally came from. As a kid, I'd lost a couple of friendships that way. One of the worst scenarios is when my father invites me to an important business dinner, and I shake hands with his potential partner. It is common practice for people to use illusion magic to hide their flaws, and I have embarrassed more than my fair share of guests by exposing their true faces. I think my father appreciates this because it sets him up for a "we all have nothing to hide" routine.

I say all of this to illustrate that I have to be especially careful when I conduct my magical research. I walked back to the door of the lab and pulled my work apron and gloves off the hook. They are made of dragonhide, which is one of the most resilient substances in all of Galevyn. It also possesses the convenient ability of suppressing my anti-magic field on the parts of my body it covers. I could commission a full-body suit, but that would hinder my movement too much, and I couldn't really do my research. Dragonhide is heavy, and it isn't the most flexible material, just the gloves and apron are hard enough to work in.

Finally, I walked over to my dragonhide-lined cabinet to pull out the necessary magic items. First things first, I slide my essentials into my front apron pocket. There's a shock ring I use for self-defense, just in case. There's a small crystal imbued with divination magic that allows my allies to track me in emergencies. Then I just had to find my jar of pure creation magic, and I could get started. I picked up the jar and was disappointed at the weight of it. It felt empty, I'd apparently used all of it the last time I worked on this. I'll have to pick up some more from the magic distillery.

I put the large jar under my arm, closed the cabinet, and walked towards the exit. On my way out, I scooped up a satchel of gold pieces to make sure I didn't have to charge anything to my father's account. If this research was going to mean anything, I was going to have to do it without his help.

"Good morning, Miss Celeste," greeted Nawha, the Orc guard my father hired to protect the mansion. Sometimes I think he actually hired her to keep track of me, specifically.

"Good morning, Nawha," I walked past her towards the door. "I'm stepping out to refill my canister of creation magic. I should be back in about an hour."

I really shouldn't have revealed to her what I was getting. My father will inevitably ask me what I'm working on, and I'll have to lie to make sure he doesn't take credit for yet another of my discoveries.

Nawha stepped in front of me to block my path, holding out her hands for my jar. "I can take care of that, Miss Celeste. No need for you to leave the premises."

"Thank you, but please, I would enjoy the morning walk," I was hoping she was in a good mood this morning and would afford me this one luxury.

Nawha grimaced. "Very well, I will inform your father if you do not return in two hours. Have a pleasant walk."

I nodded in her direction. "Of course, thank you."

I knew my father paid her to check up on me, but it felt really grating how he always wanted to know exactly where I was. I wished he would just trust me a little bit.

I walked off the property and began walking down the streets of High Anglachel. As I turned my first corner, I encountered a Gnome with all the tell-tale signs of a kidnapper: dirty hands, wild eyes, a rope loosely wrapped around his head, and a rather aggressive-looking company of men, their eyes all on me.

"Don't try to resist, little Miss Magister. We've got you now!" The Gnome growled. I held back the smirk I wanted to make at a Gnome calling a human 'little.'

"Great, another kidnapping," I resigned. Maybe Nawha was right to check up on me. This time.

www.ingramcontent.com/pod-product-compliance
Lightning Source LLC
Chambersburg PA
CBHW061433160726
47995CB00003B/869